Beecoming
Sophie™

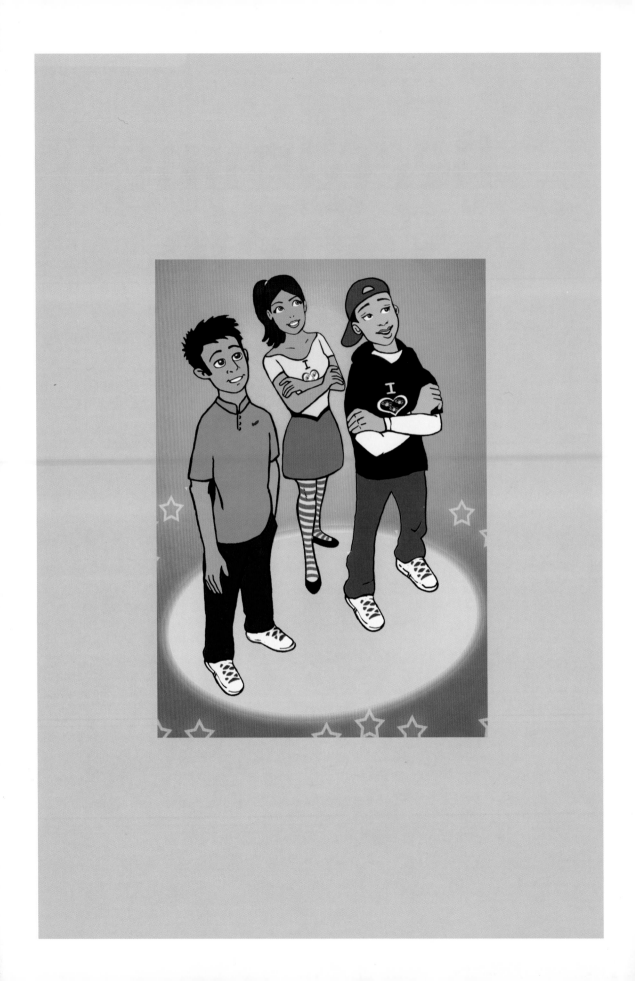

Beecoming Sophie ™

Story
Susan West Kurz

Adapted by
Mark Ellis

Art, Colors, Lettering
Melissa Martin-Ellis

**Bee Consciousness Sequence
Pencils & Inks**
Jeff Slemons

Colors
Melissa Martin-Ellis

Art Assists
Lois Keller & Deirdre DeLay Pierpoint

Cover
Sandy Littell

Special thanks to Clifford Kurz

Beecoming Sophie ™
Written by Susan West Kurz
Adapted by Mark Ellis
Illustrated by Melissa Martin-Ellis
&
Jeff Slemons

Thanks to Lois Keller and Deirdre DeLay Pierpoint

Cover by Sandy Littell

First Printing
December 2011

Deluxe Edition
April 2012

ISBN:9780983525219

Published by

Bee Conscious Publishing, Inc.
56 Wright Lane
Jamestown, RI 02835

Introduction

I hope readers enjoy *Beecoming Sophie* as much as I enjoyed writing it. The process of writing my first graphic novel and becoming a beekeeper at the same time has been fun and educational. I learned that we all feel abandoned at times in our lives and we are all guilty of abandonment, as well. It appears that we have abandoned the earth, the human community, and a connection to our own soul lives. It has been my experience that when we adopt, whether a corner of the earth, a cause, or a human being, and nurture and love them, we are nurtured ourselves.

My goal is to use this book as a platform to create a community of 500,000 new backyard Biodynamic beekeepers and bee buddies. If half a million new beekeepers have two to ten hives, or find new beekeepers in their neighborhood to achieve this total, we could restore the population of honeybees to where it was before they started disappearing in the 1970s. In the last several years we've lost about 30% of the honeybee population for a variety of reasons, Colony Collapse Disorder being a major symptom of the threat to their future.

Everyone can help the bees somehow, whether it is by purchasing local honey, planting flowers and shrubs that honeybees enjoy, or simply by stopping the use of poisonous fertilizers and pesticides on our lawns. If we take back our yards and create safe havens for the honeybees, we might find that the world will be a little sweeter.

Susan West Kurz
Jamestown, RI
December, 2011

Chapter
One

FROM SOPHIE'S JOURNAL

As I did my hair this afternoon, I danced and mouthed the words to my new favorite song, "I Miss You." I'll be performing it Friday at the lunchtime talent hour at school.

Some kids probably think the song is about a boy but it's really about my birth mother, who lives very, very far away.

I took the scrunchies out to let my hair hang loose, then I noticed a soft rain had begun to fall.

One of the screens in my room had fallen to the ground when I pushed it open one day.

Rain is one of my favorite things, I really love catching raindrops on my tongue during a storm.

I love all of nature, it is so beautiful here in Rhode Island.

I picked up my book, and the letter that I had hoped to read to my class earlier that day in school fell out.

I wasn't sure whether to read the book or reread the letter, when suddenly, I was distracted-- something flew in my window.

A BEE!!

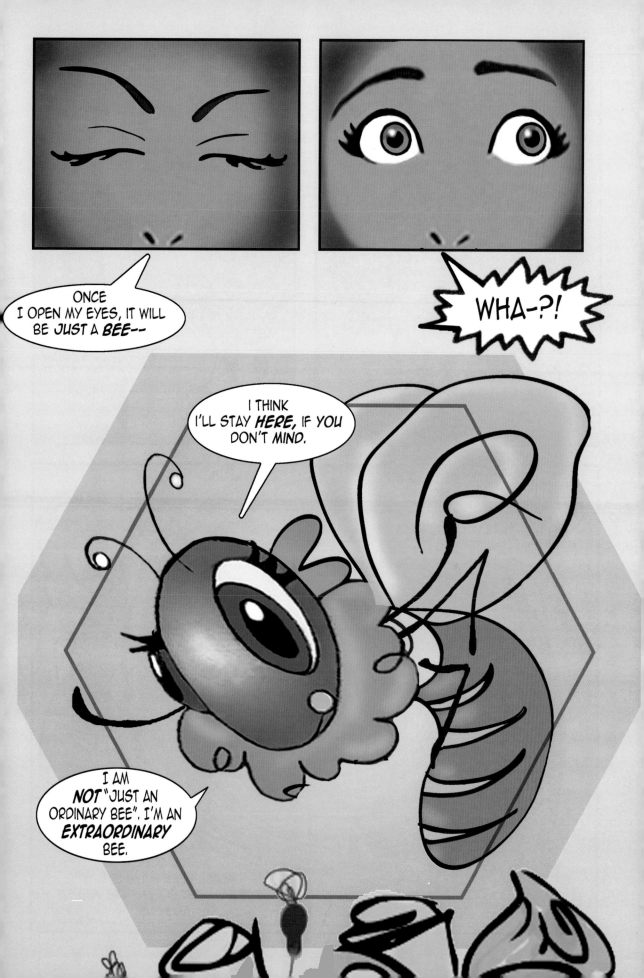

WHEN I WAS BORN, I DIDN'T WANT TO DRIVE THE OLD QUEEN AWAY FROM THE HIVE. SHE TOLD ME THAT I WOULD HAVE TO EVENTUALLY BUT THAT IT WAS A SIGN TO HER THAT I WAS THE BEE THAT ONLY COMES ALONG ONCE IN A CENTURY. THE OLD QUEEN TOLD ME THAT I WOULD KNOW EVERYTHING THERE WAS TO KNOW ABOUT BEES SINCE THE BEGINNING OF TIME.

IT WAS A GIFT AND A BURDEN.

WHAT DOES THAT MEAN? I ASKED.

I WOULD BE THE BEE THAT KNOWS HOW SPECIAL BEES ARE. I THOUGHT THE OLD QUEEN WAS KIND OF SILLY, BECAUSE EVERYONE KNOWS HOW SPECIAL BEES ARE. BUT THAT'S ALL CHANGING.

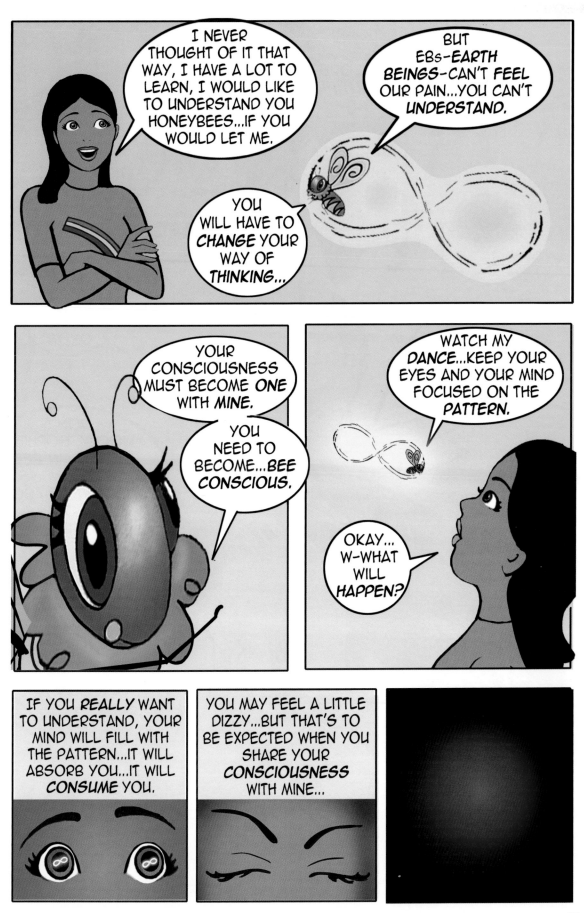

Chapter
Two

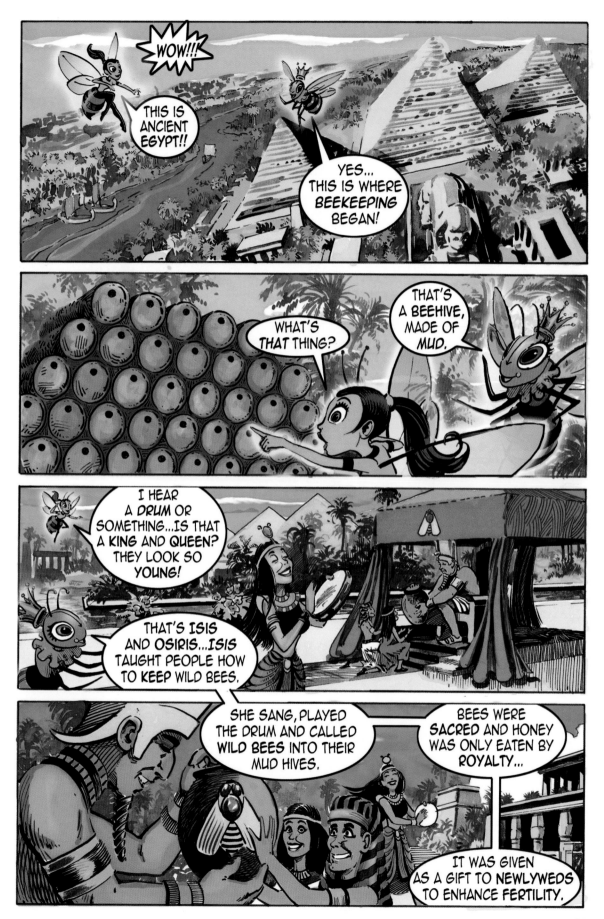

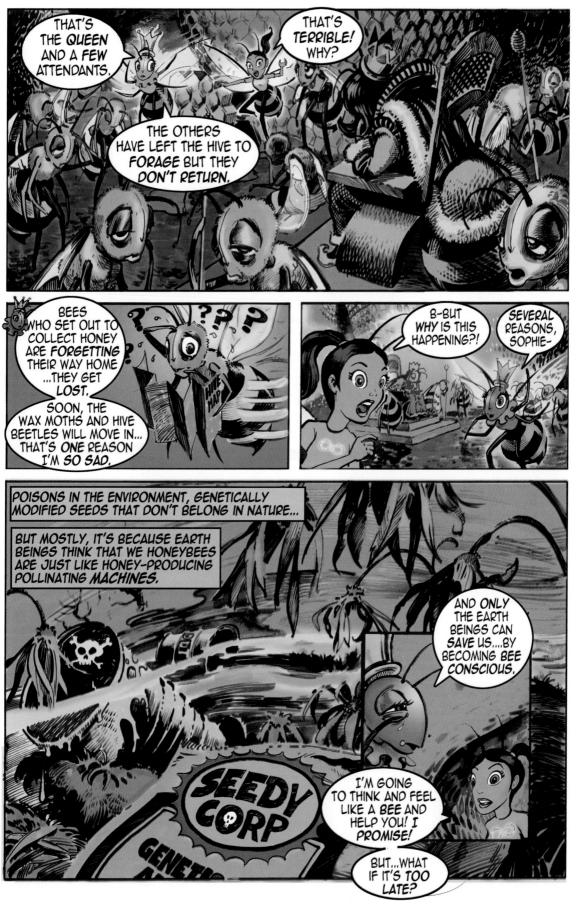

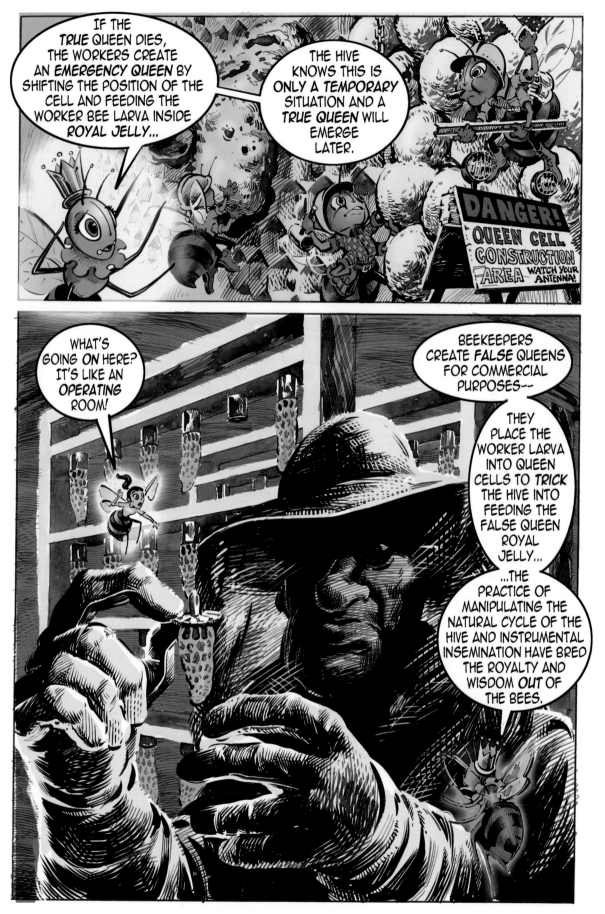

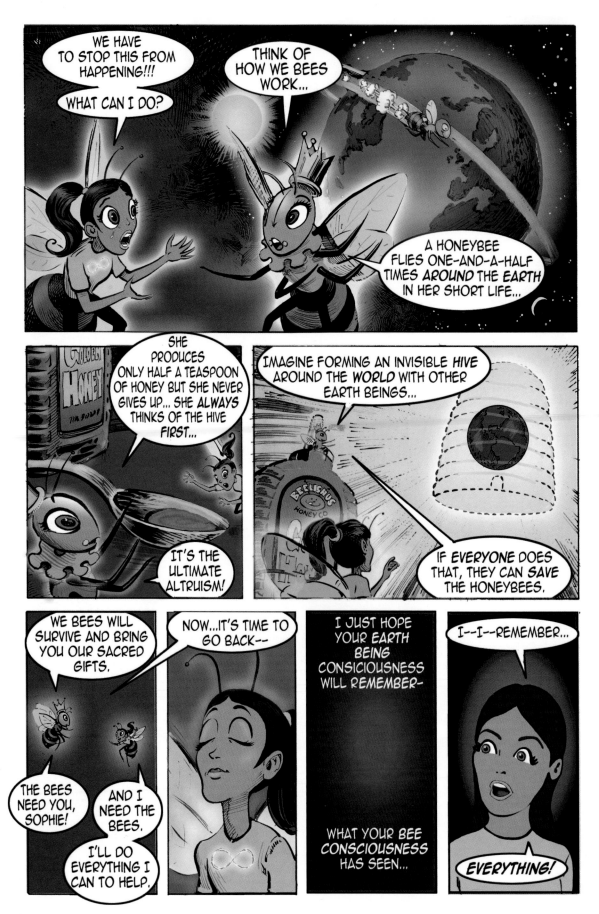

BEES DOING THE *WAGGLE DANCE*

THE MAIN SOURCES OF THE HONEYBEE'S FOOD, POLLEN AND NECTAR, DIFFER WIDELY DEPENDING ON LOCAL GEOGRAPHY, THE SEASONS AND THE TYPE OF VEGETATION AVAILABLE.

BEES COMMUNICATE THE DIRECTIONS TO FOOD SOURCES TO EACH OTHER BY MEANS OF THE ROUND DANCE AND THE *WAGGLE DANCE*.

THE FORAGING AREA AROUND A BEEHIVE USUALLY EXTENDS FOR AROUND *TWO MILES*, ALTHOUGH BEES HAVE BEEN KNOWN TO FORAGE *TWICE* AND EVEN *THREE TIMES* THIS DISTANCE FROM THE HIVE IF THE RIGHT PLANTS AREN'T READILY AVAILABLE.

UNFORTUNATELY, FORAGING AT SUCH EXTREME DISTANCES *WEARS OUT* THE WINGS OF THE BEES, AND THEREFORE *REDUCES* THE LIFE EXPECTANCY OF THE BEES IN THE COLONY.

OVER *17,000 SQUARE MILES* OF THE UNITED STATES ARE DEVOTED TO GOLF COURSES, WHICH IS AN AREA ROUGHLY EQUAL TO THAT OF *TEN* RHODE ISLANDS. RHODE ISLAND'S TOTAL AREA IS ONLY 1545 SQUARE MILES --AND 500 OF THAT IS WATER.

Chapter
Three

I dreamt of a life as a queen in a foreign land, with servants who poured warm honey over my body to keep my skin young and beautiful.

The sun spread over my bed, and suddenly, I remembered **Phoebee** and my meeting the night before with the queen bee.

ER...THAT'S A **LONG** STORY, SYLVI...HEY, HERE'S SOME STUFF ABOUT BEE STING ALLERGIES--

THAT'S WHAT MY **MOM** IS **SO** WORRIED ABOUT.

ER-- I'M **ALLERGIC** TO BEES!

AW, YOU'RE ALLERGIC TO THE **PLANET**, KEVIN!

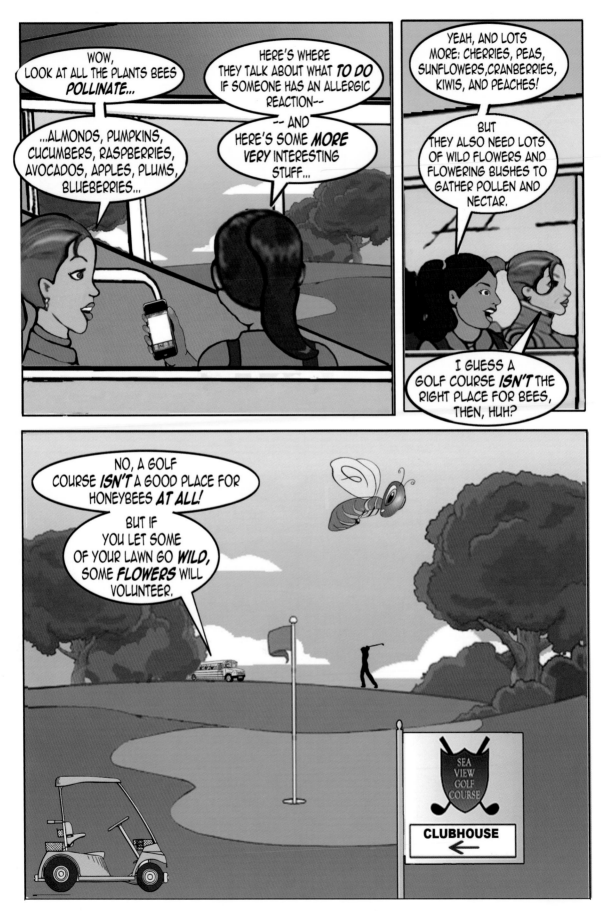

NOW DON'T GO GETTING *MODEST* ON ME. I KNOW YOU'RE SPECIAL. EVERYONE THINKS YOU'RE A *WORKER* BEE, BUT I KNOW *BETTER.*

WHEN IT STARTED *RAINING,* I DECIDED TO SPEND THE NIGHT IN AN EARTH BEING'S HOUSE. WE *ALL* NEED TO WORK TOGETHER TO *SAVE* THE BEES, THE EARTH BEINGS, AND OUR BEAUTIFUL EARTH.

AN *EARTH BEING'S* HOUSE? I'M SURPRISED YOU DIDN'T GET KILLED! DID THEY TRY TO BEAT YOU WITH A STICK OR SPRAY *POISON* ON YOU?

THEY'RE SO STUPID *AFRAID* OF BEES. THEY CAN'T TELL US APART FROM WASPS! I FIND IT VERY *INSULTING* THAT THEY THINK *WE'RE* WASPS. AS FAR AS I'M CONCERNED, HONEYBEES ARE THE *ROYALTY* OF THE INSECT WORLD!

AND I DON'T *APPRECIATE* BEING MISTAKEN FOR A *WASP!*

NOW JB, YOU KNOW THAT THERE ARE MANY *DIFFERENT* BEES RESPONSIBLE FOR BEGINNING THE LIFE PROCESSES IN SPRING—ALL *VERY* IMPORTANT. AND NO ONE TRIED TO KILL ME. IT WAS A *DIFFERENT KIND* OF EARTH BEING'S HOUSE.

DIFFERENT?

NO STRANGE LIGHTS *OR* WEIRD CURRENTS RADIATING FROM IT. THERE WAS AN *EB* GIRL, NAMED *SOPHIE* WHO LIVES THERE, I DISCOVERED SHE CAN *TALK* TO ME.

SO NOW YOU'RE COMMUNICATING WITH AN *EARTH BEING?*

YES, SHE'S AN *EB,* BUT I FEEL SHE'S ABOUT TO DISCOVER THAT SHE'S A *SPIRIT* EARTH-BEING AND THAT SHE HAS A *CONNECTION* TO NATURE.

SOPHIE WANTS TO *ADOPT* ME AND HELP SAVE THE BEES. SHE WAS ABANDONED BY HER MOTHER, WHO WAS TOO YOUNG TO CARE FOR HER—BUT SOME OTHER *EBs* ADOPTED HER, AND NOW SHE HAS A *HOME.*

AFTER PHOEBEE LEFT, JB STOPPED TO VISIT HIS FRIENDS IN THE DRONE ASSEMBLY AREA. THEY WERE DOING THEIR DAILY DRILLS, WHILE THEY KEPT LOOKOUT FOR A QUEEN TO EMERGE FROM THE HIVE AND MAKE HER LOVE FLIGHT.

WHEN A QUEEN IS READY TO MATE, SHE FLIES TOWARDS THE SUN AS FAST AS SHE CAN. THE DRONES CHASE HER--THEY ALL WANT TO BE THE FIRST TO REACH THE QUEEN IN HER LOVE FLIGHT-- THEY KNOW THAT ALTHOUGH THEY WILL DIE AFTER MATING, THEY WILL HAVE AN HONORABLE DEATH.

JB WAS TRYING TO CONVINCE THEM THAT THEIR OPTIONS AS DRONES WEREN'T OPTIMAL.

THINK OF IT... WE ONLY HAVE *THREE* CHOICES: *SUICIDAL SEX*, IF WE'RE LUCKY, *EVICTION* BY SUMMER'S END, OR *EXECUTION*, IF THE WORKERS ARE FEELING A LITTLE *CRANKY*.

DON'T YOU THINK WE SHOULD AT LEAST GET *MORE RESPECT* AND ALL THE *HONEY* WE WANT WHILE WE'RE ALIVE?

SOME DRONES GATHERED AROUND JB, HUMMING AND BUZZING IN CONSTERNATION BUT EVENTUALLY RETURNED TO THEIR DRILLS AND LOOK-OUT MODE.

JB REALIZED THAT CONVINCING THEM WOULD TAKE A VERY LONG TIME, SO HE BID HIS FRIENDS FAREWELL, JUST IN CASE ANY OF THEM WERE *GONERS* BEFORE HIS NEXT VISIT.

JB THEN MADE HIS USUAL TOUR OF THE ISLAND HIVES, LOOKING FOR ANY NEW GOSSIP. HIS FRIEND FANNIE, THE FANNER, HAD HEARD FROM FLO, THE FORAGER, THAT THERE WERE NEW HIVES ACROSS THE BAY, AT THE UNIVERSITY BAY CAMPUS.

STRANGE THINGS WERE HAPPENING. BEES WERE BEING HELD PRISONERS IN TEST TUBES AND EXPERIMENTED ON.

THE WEST BAY PASSAGE WAS FILLED WITH SAILBOATS AND JB HITCHED A RIDE HALFWAY ACROSS ON TOP OF A BRIGHT, WHITE SAIL.

THE UNIVERSITY HIVES WERE EASY TO SPOT IN A LARGE CLOVER FIELD. JB FLEW AS CLOSE AS POSSIBLE TO THE HIVES AND LANDED ON A CLOVER FLOWER NEAR THEM.

THERE WAS A **GROUP** OF EBs STANDING AROUND THE HIVES. THE BIGGEST EB WAS **TALKING** TO A GROUP GATHERED AROUND HIM.

WELL, STUDENTS, BEES ARE **VERY** INTERESTING AND SOON WE'LL KNOW **EVERYTHING** ABOUT THEM...

...LIKE THE JOKE SAYS, SOON WE'LL KNOW SO **MUCH** ABOUT BEES THAT WE WON'T **NEED** 'EM ANYMORE. HA! HA! WITH INSTRUMENTAL INSEM- INATION, **WE** CAN BREED ANY KIND OF QUEEN WE WANT!

JB TWITCHED ON THE CLOVER--HE DIDN'T FIND THE JOKE FUNNY AND WONDERED IF THAT'S WHAT PHOEBEE MEANT ABOUT FALSE QUEENS. MAYBE INSTRUMENTAL INSEMINATION HAD SOMETHING TO DO WITH IT...

THE PROFESSOR NOTICED A TALL CLOVER FLOWER TWITCHING AMONG THE GRASSES.

LOOK CLASS, THERE'S A *DRONE.*

SEE HOW MUCH *THICKER* HE IS THAN THE LONG QUEEN AND SHORTER WORKERS?

MUCH NOSIER, TOO, BUT *DRONES* DON'T STING, SO *DON'T WORRY.*

JB HAD HEARD ENOUGH. HE DIDN'T THINK THAT HE WOULD EVER THINK IT POSSIBLE, BUT HE WISHED HE WERE A WORKER BEE AT THIS MOMENT, SO HE COULD STING THE BIG PROFESSOR.

WAIT 'TILL I TELL *PHOEBEE* WHAT I HEARD TODAY-- INSTRUMENTALLY INSEMINATED BEES AND NOT NEEDING *DRONES!*

THIS IS JUST *CRAZY!*

SOME BEEKEEPERS DON'T *LIKE* DRONES BECAUSE THEY EAT SO MUCH *HONEY* AND DON'T PRODUCE *ANY.*

WHY, WITH ALL OUR SCIENTIFIC *KNOW-HOW,* WE MAY NOT EVEN *NEED* DRONES SOMEDAY. *HA HA.*

JB MADE A BEELINE BACK TO THE ISLAND AND HIS HIVE, LOOKING FOR PHOEBEE.

I WAS WATCHING THE NEW FORAGERS PRACTICE THE WAGGLE DANCE. THEY WERE ALMOST READY TO LEAVE THE HIVE AND FORAGE FOR POLLEN AND NECTAR.

THE WAGGLE DANCE IS HOW THE FORAGERS COMMUNICATE THE LOCATION AND DISTANCE OF FLOWERS FROM THE HIVE TO EACH OTHER. I LOVED THE DANCE AND USED IT AS THERAPY WHENEVER I WAS FEELING CONFUSED OR SAD.

JB WATCHED AS I CIRCLED COUNTERCLOCKWISE, THEN CLOCKWISE AND SHIMMIED WHERE THE CIRCLES OVERLAPPED. IT WAS HIS FAVORITE PART.

WHY DO *YOU* WAGGLE, PHOEBEE? *YOU* DON'T FORAGE.

WE *RESONATE* WITH THE WISDOM OF THE LIGHT.

I THINK ALL THOSE FUNNY PHONES AND COMPUTERS THAT EBS USE ARE *INTERFERING* WITH THE SONGS THAT *GUIDE* US.

KEEPS ME IN *SHAPE* AND *CONNECTED* TO THE LIGHT AND THE WISDOM OF THE STARS.

MANY BEES ARE DISAPPEARING-- *NEVER* RETURNING TO THEIR HIVES...

...IT'S LIKE THEY'RE *FORGETTING* HOW TO BE *BEES!*

YOU'RE GOING TO BE DOING IT *ALL THE TIME* WHEN I TELL YOU WHAT I HEARD TODAY!

I SAT VERY STILL AND LISTENED AS JB SPUTTERED OUT HIS STORY OF INSTRUMENTAL INSEMINATION.

MAYBE WE CAN FIND MORE EBS WHO WILL TREAT US LIKE *BEES* AND NOT *MACHINES.* I'M GOING TO VISIT *SOPHIE*--CAN I TRUST YOU WITH MY *SECRET?*

YOU CAN *TRUST* ME. WE BEES HAVE TO STICK TOGETHER. I'LL TELL *YOU* WHAT I HEAR IN THE HIVES... TELL *ME* ABOUT YOUR NEW FRIEND.

Chapter
Four

My weekly bus ride to the Adoption Network Connection meeting in Providence after school was very different from the ride to school. Tall buildings, cars, and trucks beeping their horns flashed by...but often I got to talk to interesting people, like **Mrs. Samir.**

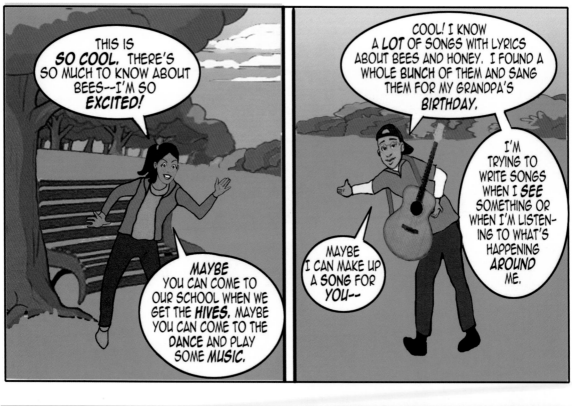

WHEN YOU'VE BEEN STUNG, WHAT ARE YOUR OPTIONS?

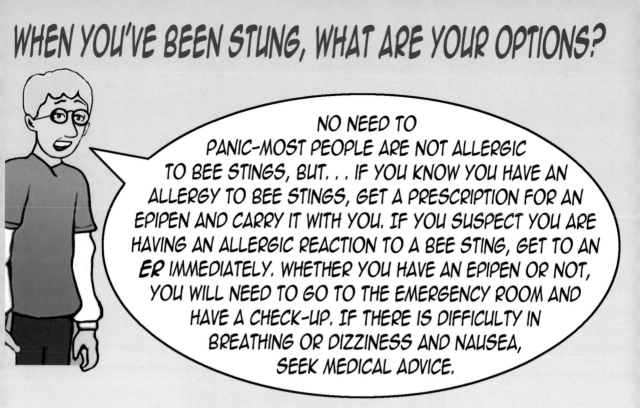

NO NEED TO PANIC-MOST PEOPLE ARE NOT ALLERGIC TO BEE STINGS, BUT. . . IF YOU KNOW YOU HAVE AN ALLERGY TO BEE STINGS, GET A PRESCRIPTION FOR AN EPIPEN AND CARRY IT WITH YOU. IF YOU SUSPECT YOU ARE HAVING AN ALLERGIC REACTION TO A BEE STING, GET TO AN **ER** IMMEDIATELY. WHETHER YOU HAVE AN EPIPEN OR NOT, YOU WILL NEED TO GO TO THE EMERGENCY ROOM AND HAVE A CHECK-UP. IF THERE IS DIFFICULTY IN BREATHING OR DIZZINESS AND NAUSEA, SEEK MEDICAL ADVICE.

ARE THERE ANY NATURAL TREATMENTS FOR BEE STINGS?

IF I HAVE BEEN STUNG, WHAT STEPS SHOULD I TAKE IF I AM NOT ALLERGIC TO BEE STINGS AND HAVE NO SYMPTOMS?

1. FOR HONEYBEES, SCRAPE THE STINGER OFF AS SOON AS YOU CAN. DO NOT PINCH IT IN ANY WAY. PINCHING SQUEEZES MORE VENOM INTO YOU.

2. ICE THE STING SITE. THIS IS THE BEST TREATMENT FOR QUICK RELIEF.

3. THE HERB, PLANTAIN, GROWS IN FIELDS AND YARDS, AND IT MAKES A GOOD EMERGENCY POULTICE FOR STINGS AND BITES. CHEW UP A COUPLE OF LEAVES AND APPLY TO THE STING.

4. HOME REMEDIES--SALT PASTE, BAKING SODA PASTE, AND MEAT TENDERIZER PASTE WILL ALL HELP DRAW OUT THE VENOM AND HELP WITH THE PAIN AND SWELLING.

5. SOME PEOPLE SWEAR BY THE HOMEOPATHIC REMEDY, APIS MELLIFICA, TO REDUCE SWELLING AND PAIN.

Chapter
Five

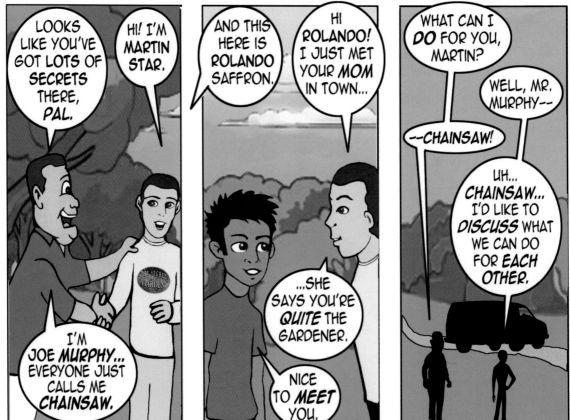

The marsh is by an inlet which leads into the bay and eventually to the ocean ... Rolando and I knew that our birth mother lived far across the ocean, in Puerto Barrios, Guatemala.

I don't really remember my mother, except as a shadowy figure, but when Rolando and I were younger, we wrote messages to her, saying we'd always love her, and would come visit her someday.

We placed the messages in bottles and threw them into the marsh at high tide, hoping they would eventually reach the Pacific ... and our mother.

In this place, thoughts of bees, my birth mother, wildflowers and boys all buzzed through my head.

I CALLED **MOM**...SHE'LL PICK US UP IN A FEW MINUTES.

WHAT'S SO IMPORTANT? WHO'S PHOEBEE?

WELL... SHE'S A HONEY BEE!

A HONEY BEE?!?

NOT AN **ORDINARY** BEE...SHE CAN **TALK!** AND I CAN TALK TO HER--

...AND SO SHE **FLEW AWAY** THIS MORNING, BUT IT'S BECAUSE OF **HER** I KNOW ALL THIS STUFF ABOUT **BEES** AND I'M FINDING OUT SO MUCH **MORE** ON THE INTERNET AND WE HAVE TO DO **SOMETHING!**

DO YOU **BELIEVE** ME?

A TALKING BEE...

UH... I **DUNNO**.... I MEAN, EVEN IF I DO, **SO WHAT?**

YOU CAN HELP ME WITH **MOM**... SAY YOU'LL TAKE CARE OF PLANTING THE **FLOWERS** THAT **PHOEBEE** TOLD ME ABOUT.

WE DON'T NEED SUCH A BIG LAWN ANYWAY, EXCEPT TO PLAY BALL ON, RIGHT?

THAT'S FOR SURE...TAKES ME **HOURS** TO CUT IT.

SO, YOU **DO BELIEVE** ME?

I **GUESS.** BUT--

BEEP-A-BEEP!

THERE'S MOM!

Chapter
Six

78

SOPHIE, WATCH ME CLOSELY!

CAN I LEARN TO DO THAT?

Phoebee circled around me and I followed her movements with my eyes.

THIS IS THE WAGGLE DANCE. IT'S HOW BEES TELL THE HIVE IN WHAT DIRECTION AND HOW FAR TO FLY TO FIND FLOWERS...

...IT ALSO HELPS KEEP WORKERS FINE-TUNED AND CONNECTED TO THEIR INTELLIGENCE, SOPHIE!

PHOEBEE, PLEASE SHOW ME HOW TO DO THE WAGGLE DANCE!

HOLD UP THAT WING...ER, I MEAN ARM!

THIS ONE, MY LEFT ONE?

YES! THEN MAKE A BIG CIRCLE AND FOLLOW IT AROUND UNTIL YOU GET BACK TO WHERE YOU STARTED.

THEN LEAD WITH THE OTHER ARM, AND CIRCLE BACK TO THE BEGINNING...

...THEN SHAKE AND SHIMMY LIKE THIS!

I began moving in alternating circles, going faster and faster...

THAT'S SO COOL. MY ARM IS ON THE INSIDE OF THE CIRCLE FIRST, THEN ON THE OUTSIDE WHEN I GO THE OTHER WAY. I'M GOOD AT THIS!

WHAT'S INSIDE GOES OUT AND WHAT'S OUTSIDE GOES IN. IT'S LIKE A RIDDLE. I'M NOT EVEN GETTING DIZZY!

83

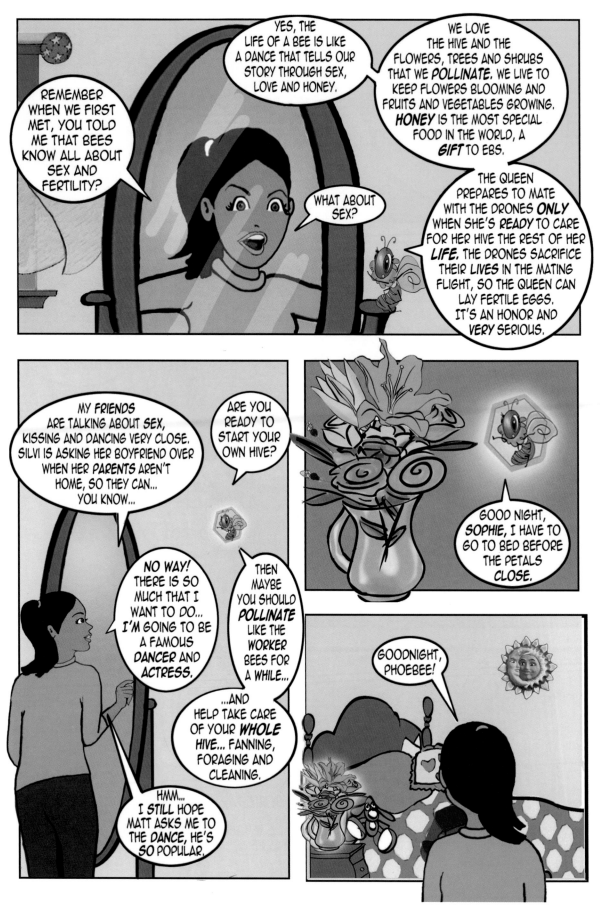

Chapter
Seven

We peddled slowly, changing into the lowest gears as we rode up the steady incline to the highest part of the island to the Seaview Golf Course.

THE SECOND TRIP WILL BE *EASIER*, WE'LL ONLY HAVE TO CARRY 50 LBS. EACH...

WHATEVER... I'LL FEEL A *LOT BETTER* WHEN THIS IS DONE AND WE'RE BACK IN BED.

IT'S *LUCKY* I HAVE THE KEY...

SEAVIEW GOLF COURSE

MEMBERS ONLY

The shed was stacked high wiith grass seeds the course uses, purchased from the Seedy Corporation.

SEEDY CORPORATION

ROGUE SEED

WARNING: DO NOT USE IF:
Pregnant or nursing; suffering from any respiratory condition; asthma, emphysema, bronchitis.

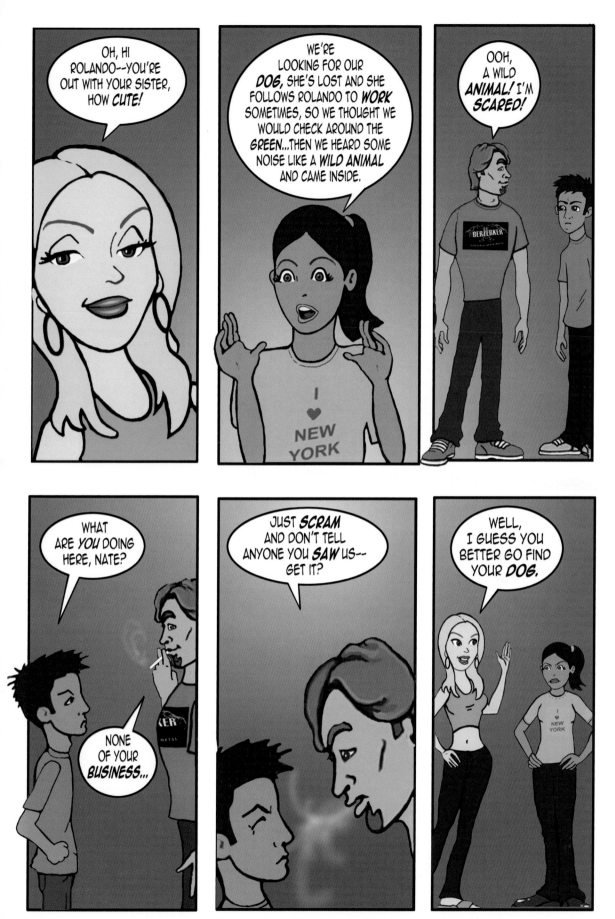

Chapter
Eight

Chapter
Nine

102

Chapter
Ten

AN ART TREE WOULD BE SO COOL...RECYCLED BOTTLES, CRYSTALS AND CDS CAN MAKE ANY TREE INTO A MAGICAL PLACE TO SIT UNDER AND ENJOY NATURE.

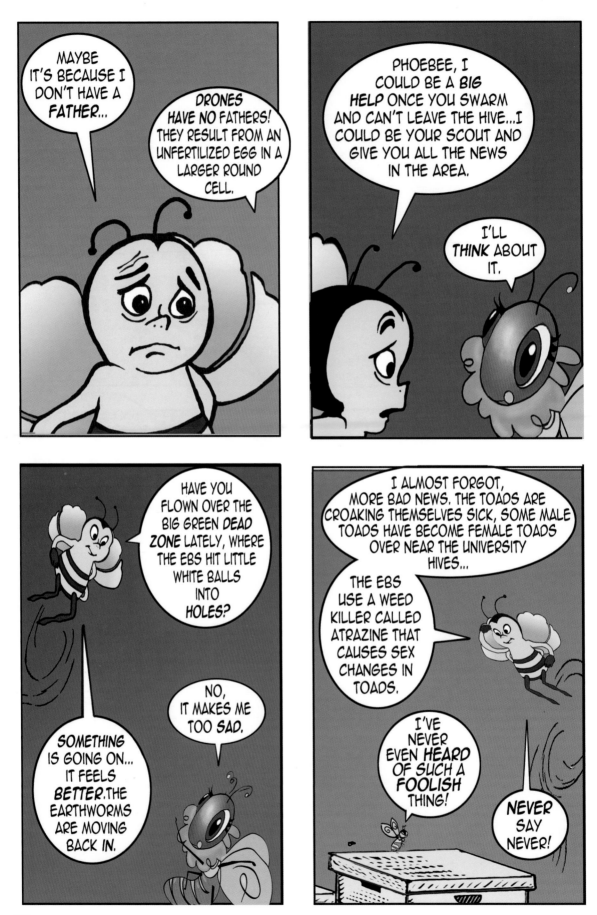

Chapter
Eleven

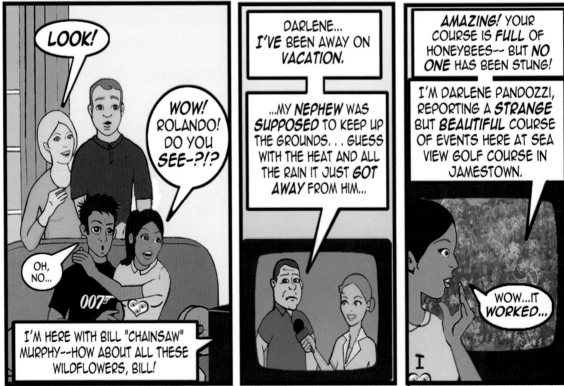

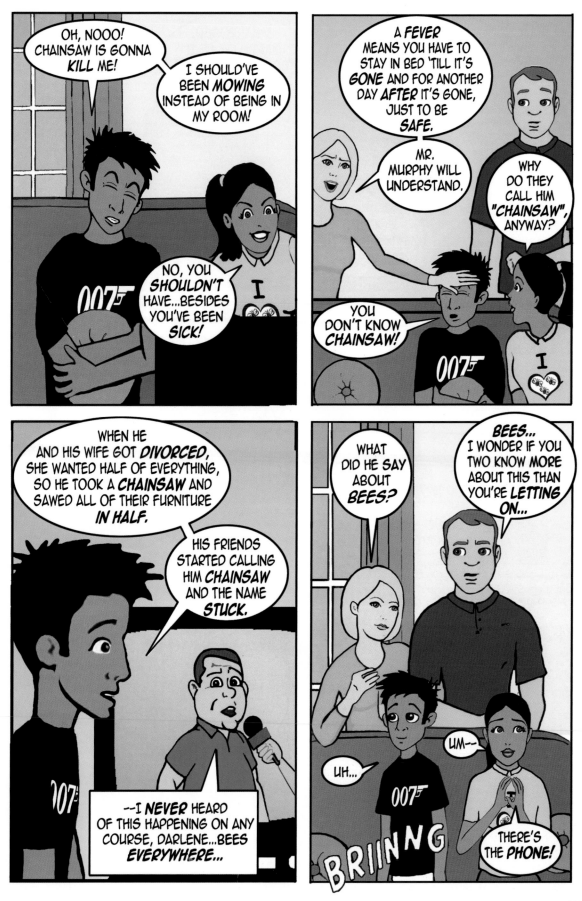

113

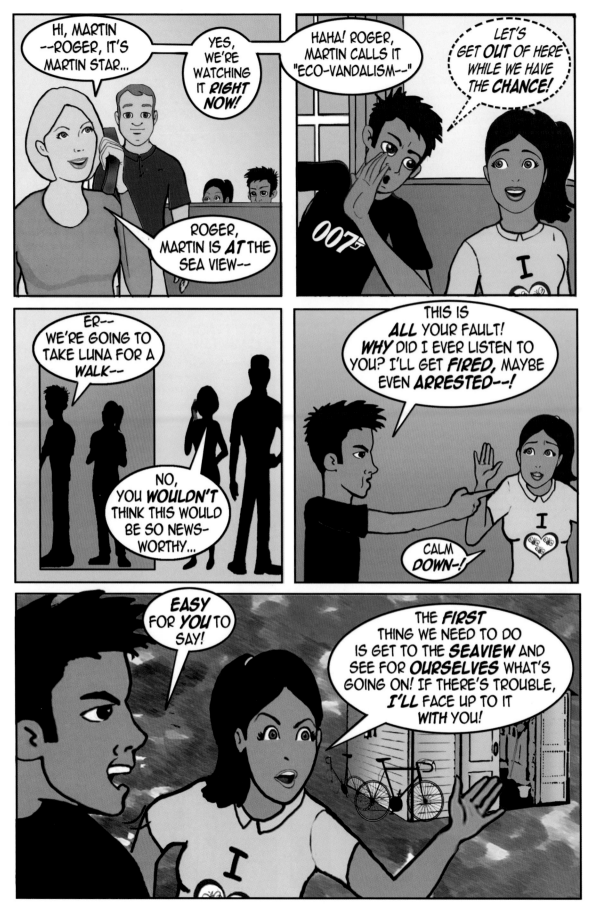

120

124

128

Chapter
Twelve

I reread Mama Rosita's recent letter and realized she writes similar letters each year.

Dear Children,

I send my warmest wishes and hope that you are happy and healthy.

I write this letter because I want to keep in communication with you.

Each day I think of you and pray that I made the right decision to find a good home for you.

My dream is that I will see you again someday and you will be healthy and that you will find happiness.

Good Bye and many hellos,

Rosita

I TOLD MOM I'D GET UP EARLY AND WEED THE FLOWER BED...

BUT I HAVE TO DO SOMETHING FOR MY BIRTH MOTHER AS WELL. MAMA ROSITA, I WANT YOU TO BE PART OF WHAT I'M DOING FOR THE BEES.

SO I'M PLANTING YOUR LOVING LETTER IN MY BEE GARDEN.

IN THE FALL, I'LL PLANT CROCUSES AND SNOWDROPS HERE. AND MAYBE I'LL VISIT YOU...

...WHEN I'M OLDER AND CAN SPEAK *SPANISH*. I'LL SHOW YOU HOW TO START A *BEEHIVE*.

SOPHIE--

PHOEBEE! YOU'RE BACK! I'M *SO* GLAD!

I CAME TO SEE YOU BEFORE I GO BACK TO MY HIVE AS *THE QUEEN*.

My To-Do List is getting out of control!

Dad organized his home brew club to make honey beer and mead to sell at the August dance...

With Mr. Murphy's blessing, we're holding two dances at Sea View instead of one...

Mom rolls her eyes when he says things like, "The real strength of honey is that it adds potency to beer, yet smooths out the bitter edge of the hops."

The teens-only dance is set for Earth Day and the second one for all ages is scheduled for August 21st...Honeybee Awareness Day!

I get daily requests to visit schools and talk about Bee Conscious Support...I tell kids about the importance of safety when working with bees and how we need whole communities to help.

I want us to become the first Bee Conscious state in the country!

137

Soukuen asked me to create a Waggle Dance routine to the music that he composed to go with the lyrics I'd shared with him.

DO THE WAGGLE DANCE, WAKE UP FROM YOUR TRANCE...

My Jazz dance instructor helped me and my class work out a routine that we could all perform at the Bee on the Tee.

Rolando got a video camera as an early birthday present and he taped me and my dance class doing the Waggle Dance.

He says it's a good idea to post it on the BeeConscious.com website that he wants to build --and maybe even put it on YouTube!

The tickets to the dance sold out quickly. When the donations and matching funds from Doris Beaufort began to arrive, Mr. Murphy wondered if maybe we should have one of these every month!

The night of the dance finally arrived!

Mom and Dad drove me and Rolando to Sea View early so we could line the driveway to the club house with luminaria....paper bags filled with sand with a candle in each one.

In the beautiful spring twilight, the place looked magical...not like a golf course at all.

SEA VIEW GOLF COURSE
BEE ON THE TEE DANCE TONIGHT!

Sokuen, his uncle, cousin and three friends arrived in a van filled with instruments and speakers for the musicians and the DJ.

Mr. Murphy sure seemed relieved when they showed up!

Mom decorated the community room with flowers, jars of honey, and balloons.

She and her knitting group had volunteered to knit and sell felted flowers to raise money for the course.

BEE ON THE TEE DANCE TONIGHT!

According to Mr. Murphy, the place had never looked so good!

I saw Queen Phoebee circle and shimmy in a figure eight high above us, as she flew away toward the setting sun.

The Queen

Hey Soapy,

I was thinking about bees and the queen after our talk today, so I asked my granddad about it...he's a master beekeeper. Now I'm beginning to understand why you're so excited about helping the bees.

My grandfather—The Grandman — told me that a queen can lay 500-2,000 eggs a day, more weight-wise than her own body weight! That's pretty incredible!

Granddad said: "She lays eggs in those beautifully constructed hexagonal cells and worker bees are created. The hex cells for drones are larger, and when the queen puts her abdomen into such a cell, she puts an unfertilized egg into it. Worker bees come from fertilized cells."

Man, oh man! That's virgin birth for a drone! So I wanted to know how does she know when to lay an unfertilized egg. Granddad laughed and told me, "She just feels the difference. No brainwork, college degree, or exams necessary."

So now I was really curious about how a new queen is made. Maybe in a cell lined with gold and gems...

Granddad shook his head. "Oh, come on! You'll never guess! It's the same egg as for a worker, but there are four important differences for an egg to become a queen: substance, position, form and time."

"I don't get it," I said. "Most beekeepers don't get it either, and that's a huge problem," Grandman told me. "The time to mature, 16 days for a queen versus 21 days for a worker, is a given fact. Aside from that, beekeepers only consider substance—royal jelly—to be of importance. The queen-to-be, as soon as she becomes a larva on the 3rd day, gets fed royal jelly. So do the worker larvae, but she gets to swim in a denser, protein-rich jelly and receives that throughout her larval state; the workers only for a day or two."

So I was like, "Wow, she feeds with her whole body, not only with her mouth?"

Grandman said, "Yeah, that's right. It's like sunbathing for us. We soak in the sunlight and make nourishment. We all need, Vitamin D. The bees soak in the liquid food, which actually is transformed sunlight—nectar and pollen."

He went on to explain that position and form isn't something we're trained to observe and notice. American Indians and other cultures trained to gain knowledge, not only with the head, but also through subtle perceptions, with their entire body. That's a lot better for understanding such things. The longer you're around bees, the more you learn from them. According to Granddad, worker and drone cells are positioned in a horizontal plane, whereas the queen cell is facing straight down.

I couldn't see why that made a difference and the Grandman said, "Look, a psychiatrist will let a patient lie on a couch. He wouldn't get the same information if the patient stood or sat up. And when you want to feel real important, feel the "I am Sokuen", feel the king in you, you stand up straight. You don't slouch back and lie in your chair. Royalty, the queen, needs the perpendicular plane! You could also put it this way: you want to look up to a queen or king. They represent a deity on Earth."

So I said, "Wow! And to think the bees know this."

The Grandman just smiled. "That's what is called instinct, Son. Every animal actually brings tremendous wisdom down to the Earth."

I was really curious about the form stuff and why it's so important and he explained, "I told you that workers and drones develop in hexagonal cells. Well, queens develop in roundish cells. First, it's a cup like the cap on an acorn. When the cell is finished, it looks like a hanging peanut."

I asked why and the Grandman answered, "The famous poet and scientist Goethe said that nature is an open secret. We see the tree, the stone, and the animal but in each, there is a deep secret hidden. All I know is that nests are round and give equal warmth to all sides. And I also know that each geometric form has a different sound, a force field. I guess the queen just needs a lot of roundness in her early stages so she can be really alive, have the tremendous life forces necessary to lay all those eggs each day. It is also a mystery that the queen hatches in 16 days while the worker takes 21 and the drone 24! In a little over two weeks, the princess is finished and all she needs to be a queen is to go on a marriage flight. About 4-6 days after she hatches from the cell, she goes on a marriage or nuptial flight, up to a height of 600 feet, where a dozen or so drones mate with her—and die. Then she has enough sperm to last throughout her lifetime."

Then the Grandman got kind of serious and told me that the way we've been breeding queens for the last 100 years is one of the biggest problems facing the bees. So I asked, "How are the queens bred?"

Granddad said, "We discovered--toward the end of the 19th century--that the bees can make an emergency queen out of a worker larva if the queen suddenly dies. The workers can take a young worker larva, the younger the better, change the shape and position of the cell and feed her royal jelly the last few days of larval development. Somehow, the colony knows that a queen raised out of a worker larva isn't quite royal enough and this so-called emergency queen is replaced by a real queen the same year or the following year. The colony then raises a real queen, and that means that from the very beginning, from the minute the egg was deposited, that queen has been in the right cell form and position.

"So, we found out that we can copy that emergency situation. We remove the queen from the hive, put worker larvae into pre-fab queen cups and raise 30-40 queens at one time. Big business, big bucks!"

I asked, "But is it really so bad that we raise queens this way?"

Grandman looked at me like I'd asked a really stupid question. "Sokuen, when we manipulate nature like that, we don't see the negative effect for a long time. But by now, it's clear that after so many generations, the cumulative effect isn't good. Bit by bit, we have bred the royalty out of our queens. Their health and life expectancy is way down. They last anywhere from a few months to two years -- at most, half of their former life expectancy. We can't treat bees like an assembly line. You see, when we mechanize a life process, we increase quantity, but always at the cost of quality. It is essential to realize that the whole hive is one living organism. The individual bee is not the reproductive organism."

I asked, "So how do you connect this to CCD, to that huge crisis with honeybee colonies disappearing?"

Grandman had an unusual answer. He said that all the viruses, bacteria, mites and beetles, together with the lack of a diverse food supply and the stress the bees experience in being trucked around the country is only one aspect of the problem. The other aspect is that we go against their natural instincts in so many ways and that we have industrialized our beekeeping methods to the utmost. And with artificial queen breeding, we have the core of the problem. The queens have been reduced in their royalty over time, and when no real queen is at home in the hive, guess what? The bees don't have the incentive to come back and the beekeeper finds the hive empty. Of course, the poisons used now can affect the nervous system of the bees and can also be part of the whole picture.

According to the Grandman, the solutions to this problem are: more organic agriculture (i.e., no pesticides), diversified orchards with bees being kept instead of trucked in, more and more hobby beekeepers really caring for the bees, letting them swarm, create their own queens, feed on their own honey and pollen, and, most important, beekeepers who don't let the bottom-line dictate their way of keeping the bees.

So, Soapy—after everything I learned, I can see why you're so psyched about helping the bees!

Your friend,
Sokuen

Swarming

The first time our bees swarmed was a beautiful day in May. I was doing my homework in the family room, staring out the window. There, hovering in large undulating movements, were thousands of buzzing bees. I ran out shouting "Papi, come quick!"

The bees moved from the window to the front of the house. It was like they realized they had my attention and could continue their flight. We stood near the hives and watched the swirling vortex of thousands of bees concentrate their form from about thirty feet wide to about five feet. Many bees landed about 15 feet up in the old cedar tree, the rest almost 40 feet high.

"I hope they choose the lower branch to finally cluster," said Papi. We watched in awe as their dance continued, eventually ending on the higher branch.

"How are we ever going to catch them?" I wondered aloud.

"We might have to let them go."

"No way!" We have to catch them and take care of them," I said. Eventually Papi and my brother Rolando captured them using a very long extension ladder, an empty cardboard box and a very long rope. Rolando climbed the ladder and threw the rope over the branch where the bees were clustered. He held the box under the branch and Papi pulled on the ends of the rope. The branch shook and the bees fell into the box. Rolando quickly climbed down the ladder with a box full of bees. Papi poured them gently into the new hive. They repeated the process two more times before capturing almost all the bees.

There's an old saying: "A swarm in May is worth a load of hay. A swarm in June is worth a silver spoon, and a swarm in July isn't worth a fly." The logic is that if you get hold of an extra hive of bees early in the season, they'll be able to build a home and make some honey. But by July, it's too late for them to do much. In fact, many beekeepers try to prevent bees from swarming at all, because they lose half of the bees in a hive when they swarm.

Swarming often occurs when a hive is in such good shape that it needs room for egg laying and nectar storage. The bees have completed all their tasks and the cupboards are full of honey. In holistic beekeeping, swarming is a natural, reproductive process that is good for the bees. It's like giving birth to a new baby. We need more bees; they're disappearing, so swarms are good. Like a friend of Sokuen's grandfather says "It's about the bees, not about the honey!"

About half the bees in the hive, gorged with enough honey for three days accompany the old queen. When she chooses a place to land, thousands of bees begin to cluster around her to protect her. Scouts go out looking for the best place to make their new home. When negotiations are done and a final decision is made, the swarm departs. The swarm usually remains in place for four to twenty-four hours. It is a remarkable situation in that the swarm leaves the results of all of their hard work behind before they have even picked a place to go. Then back to work again when they find a new home. They start from scratch, having left their "retirement" behind for the newly born hive. They are very docile when in a swarm. If you don't catch the cluster, they fly way and hopefully find an empty tree trunk, old building or somewhere suitable to perform their magic.

Meanwhile the new queen will hatch in the old hive and soon take her nuptial flight and the rejuvenation of the hive left behind will begin.

Get to Know Your Honey Bee

In Biodynamic holistic beekeeping we think of the bees and the hive as one living organism rather than 50 to 60 thousand individual bees. The honey bee organism consists of three different types of bees: the queen, the workers, and the drones.

The queen bee is the longer, slender bee on the left. The only time she is outside of the hive is during her mating flight or when she swarms. The queen bee is a true ruler in the noblest sense: she is a servant her entire life.

Perhaps being a beekeeper should bee a prerequisite for all politicians and world leaders! The queen bee egg and larva develop in a round sack-like cell, oriented vertically, instead of the hexagonal shaped, horizontal cells of the workers. She hatches in the shortest amount of time of her coworkers: 16 days. She usually mates once in her life, high up in the air with a number of drones, accumulating enough semen to last her for several years. On a good day in May or June she can lay several thousand eggs, more than her body weight, which is a tremendous feat. The queen has an intimate and deep relationship with the workers. All of them are her progeny and she is the one that gives them a sense of belonging, the individual 'smell' of the colony.

Holistic beekeepers support the value of keeping the queen as long as she lives instead of replacing her each year as though she were a machine part. It is wonderful to look for the queen when you go into your hive to check on what is happening. She usually lives deep in the hive surrounded by her court of workers.

The smaller bee in the diagram is the worker. During the summer within one hive, for one queen, there may be as many as 50,000 to 60,000 workers. The term "labor of love" truly applies to worker bees who accomplish their work without endless meetings and emails just harmonious, resonating wisdom. All the needs of the queen are provided by the worker bees. They clean, stroke, warm or cool her depending on the weather. They nourish the queen with a secretion from glands on their head close to their mouth. It is called the royal jelly. It is the worker bee that we see buzzing happily around gathering nectar and pollen from flowers, bushes, and trees during the spring and summer. When the old queen decides to swarm, up to half of the worker bees follow her to their new home. The worker bee egg is laid in a hexagonal shaped cell which is oriented almost horizontally. It develops to an adult in about 21 days. When we see worker bees flying in warm, sunny weather, it is as though they are sunlight in flight. The worker bees accomplish phenomenal tasks and it is for that reason that Biodynamic holistic beekeepers want to provide them with sound nutrition: their own honey and pollen. A honey bee cannot eat junk food and continue to flourish in an environment that is becoming more challenged with pollution and fewer flowers.

The drone is the plump bee on the right in the illustration. These amiable and gentle males are physically the largest and heaviest of the three kinds of bees in the hive. They have much larger feelers and larger eyes than the workers. You can even hold them in your hands and they won't sting since they have no stinger. The drones need twenty-three to twenty-four days to mature from egg to adult.

Their very distinguished role within the hive seems to be limited to mating with the queen -- and not all of them will perform this task. They appear to be the opposite of worker bees: they don't work at all, they can't even feed themselves. The workers must feed them. To an observer they appear passive until just the right sunny day. Then they fly up to about 500 to 600 feet in the air, hovering in mysterious locations that attract drones from a radius as wide as eight to ten miles. The young queens fly up to these clouds of drones and beyond them. The strongest drones follow the queen and up to a dozen drones can mate with her – and die upon accomplishing their mission. Drones are without a doubt vital to the propagation of the hive.

The Biodynamic beekeepers in addition to honoring the drones for propagation also recognize the drone as sense organs for the hive. The pronounced eyes and feelers of the drones hint at skills beyond those of mating. The drones are the eyes and ears of the hive, integrating the outer world of nature with the inner wisdom of the hive. Ancient cultures and the Native Americans all recognized a 'group soul' in the animal world -- holistic beekeepers are learning that bees have an almost other-worldly nature and intelligence about them.

Types of Bees

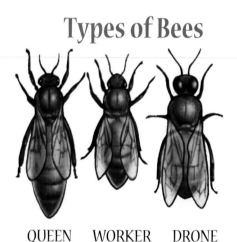

QUEEN   WORKER   DRONE

Nucs – the Nucleus of the Hive

I went with Papi to pick up our nucs from a local beekeeper. The name "nuc" kind of freaked me out because it sounds like "nuke" which is something my friends and I are afraid of. But a nuc is what you need to begin your journey as a new beekeeper. Preferably a new beekeeper can find a source of local nucs rather than nucs from Georgia. When a hive is divided to create one or more new colonies, each new hive is given a small version, or nucleus, of what is found in a full-sized hive. It's a mini version of a bee hive. So they call these artificial swarms a nucleus colony, or nuc for short. It contains: worker bees and a queen, eggs, larvae, hatching bees, pollen, and honey—all on five frames, just like in the regular hive.

When we picked up our nucs, I felt like we were coming home with a new baby. It was so exciting. After we got home Papi and Rolando carefully placed the five frames into the middle of a freshly built hive body with five more frames. When people find out how peaceful and magical honey bees are, I hope that we can replace all our nukes with nucs!

Bee Smokers & Smoking

When Papi opened our new smoker from Busybee Supplies, it reminded me of the Tin Man's oil can in the Wizard of Oz.

What you put inside the smoker is more important than the smoker itself. The goal is to produce a cool, non-acrid smoke. Professional beekeepers frequently use: burlap, bailing twine, rolled corrugated cardboard or wood shavings in the smoker.

Once, when Papi and I were on a field trip with a master beekeeper looking for native plants that bees like, we came across beehives on the edge of a local community garden. The master beekeeper approached the hives with great respect and placed his ear to them. He made sure to stand behind the hives from where bees were buzzing in and out, heading to the abundant flowers for pollen and nectar.

He gathered some dry grasses, wrapped them into a tight bunch; lit them, then blew out the flame. He fanned the smoke into the front of the hive so we could examine it. He emphasized that we should not make a smoker in this way. A proper smoker is much safer. But this was an unusual situation. He wanted us to see how friendly honeybees are and how to act around unknown bees.

That day we learned smoking the hive is the principal tool for controlling bees. It interferes with the pheromone "smell" communication "language" that the bees use to raise a "we're under attack" alarm.

Today's bees are said to have a genetic link to the time when bush fires ravaged the earth and the smell of smoke signaled them to load up on honey and move house.

The beekeeper smokes the hive for a short time, long enough for the bees to gorge themselves on honey which make them very docile and in no mood for a fight. The same is true when bees swarm--they are loaded with honey then too. So the idea of an angry swarm of bees pursuing a hapless person is far from reality. After the bees are smoked, the beekeeper can safely examine the hive and remove capped frames loaded with honey.

Acknowledgements

I would like to thank my husband Clifford for his love, edits and hands-on beekeeping skills. The day he learned I was writing a book about bees is the day he ordered our nucs, hives and enough equipment to last us for the next five years. Thanks to our three children, John West Walsh, Emilio and Rossibel Kurz and my sister Rae Nelson for all the love, support and joy they bring to me daily.

Thanks also to my son John and to Catharina Steiner for their honest feedback and "journalistic eyes". Melissa Martin-Ellis and Mark Ellis not only encouraged me to write this story as a graphic novel but showed me how to do it. The Newport Round Table Writers gave me valuable feedback when I workshopped the book and I am very grateful for all I learned from them. Sandy Littell spent countless hours designing the cover that met so many needs. I'd like to thank Lucy Hawking for her editorial feedback and encouragement. I am also grateful to Dr Hauschka Skin Care, Inc., and WALA Heilmittel GmbH for the 30 years experience I had discovering the importance of approaching health, nature, business, and human beings from a holistic world view.

I dedicate this book to the memory of Rudolf Steiner, the visionary born 150 years ago this year, who brought the gift of Anthroposophy to the world. The worldwide movement of Anthroposophic activities includes Biodynamic Agriculture, Waldorf Education, Sustainable Business Models, Anthroposophic Medicine, Healing and Performing Arts, and the Camp Hill Community for special needs, to name but a few.

Susan West Kurz

Bios

Susan West Kurz

Maurice Haas photo

Susan is a renowned holistic beauty expert, co-founder of Dr Hauschka Skin Care Inc. and author of *Awakening Beauty the Dr Hauschka Way*. From 1992 to 2006, Susan oversaw the development of Dr. Hauschka Skin Care from a modest niche company to what is now recognized as the preeminent holistic skin care brand.

Since her apprenticeship at the Meadowbrook Herb Garden in Richmond Rhode Island in 1972, Susan has been involved with a holistic approach to healing, to business and to bringing Biodynamic agriculture and gardening practices to the public. Her concern for the plight of the honeybee triggered the idea for *Beecoming Sophie* and the unique approaches suggested in the book for stopping the disappearance of the bees and for protecting our food freedom.

The family in *Beecoming Sophie* is loosely based on Susan's own family. In 2000, she and her husband Clifford adopted two Guatemalan children—a five year-old girl named Rossibel and and her seven year-old brother Emilio—and have watched them grow and flourish with much love, a holistic lifestyle and healthy food. Susan's oldest son, John West Walsh from her marriage to actor J.T. Walsh, visits the family and beehives frequently for supplies of Bee Conscious honey at their home in Jamestown, Rhode Island, between his film career and work in the recovery field.

Mark Ellis

Mark is a novelist and comics creator whose many credentials include *Doc Savage: The Man of Bronze, The Wild, Wild West, Nosferatu: Plague of Terror, The Miskatonic Project* and *Star Rangers*. Under the pen name of James Axler, he created the best-selling *Outlanders* novel series for Harlequin Enterprises' Gold Eagle imprint. Now in its fifteenth consecutive year of publication, the series has sold well over a million copies worldwide.

The author of over 50 books, Mark co-wrote, with his wife Melissa Martin-Ellis, *The Everything Guide to Writing Graphic Novels*. He has been featured in *Starlog, Comics Scene* and *Fangoria* magazines. He has also been interviewed by Robert Siegel for NPR's *All Things Considered*.

Melissa Martin-Ellis

Melissa is a professional artist, writer, graphic designer and photographer. Involved in publishing for over three decades, she co-wrote *The Everything Guide to Writing Graphic Novels* and is the author of *The Everything Guide to Photography, 101 Ways to Find a Ghost* and *The Everything Ghost Hunting Book*. Her work as a writer and photographer has appeared in *Newport Life Magazine, The Boston Globe, The Providence Journal, Newport This Week, Newport Daily News, NRT's Walls and Bridges Anthology* and *Balancing the Tides Literary Magazine*. She and her husband Mark founded and moderate The Newport Round Table Writers' Group, in Newport, Rhode Island and have taught writing workshops for Newport Round Table, The Rhode Island Writer's Circle, The Cape Cod Writers Group and The Connecticut Authors and Publishers Association.

Jeff Slemons

Jeff is a Colorado illustrator who actually received a D in high school art because he was too busy experimenting with pen and ink, gouache, watercolors, oils and mixed media to complete the assignment—drawing a kitten poking its head out of a slipper. After graduating from the Colorado Institute of Art in 1986, Jeff quickly became a sought-after illustrator for *Country Home Magazine, Golf World, The Hollow Earth Expedition Source-book,* Coca Cola and Hasbro. He shows his fine art in Houston, Vail and Denver and his work has been showcased in *Heavy Metal* magazine and *Spectrum 17: The Best in Contemporary Fantastic Art.* He is currently working on graphic novels, book covers and the occasional kitten in a slipper.

Sandy Littell

Sandy is a cover artist, graphic designer, artist, budding children's book writer, wife and mother to four great kids. Her clients have included Dr. Hauschka Skin Care, Yoga Center Amherst, Lifenet North America and many small businesses. In 2010 she received her MFA in "Writing for Children" from Simmons College at the Eric Carle Museum of Picture Book Art, in Amherst, Massachusetts. Her love for animals, gardening, good food, babies, bright colors, soft grass and wonderful friends inspires her work, and she would like to thank the honeybees of the world for their devotion to humanity in service to life on Earth.

Resources

BOOKS

Bees - Lectures by Rudolf Steiner

Toward Saving the Honeybee - by Gunther Hauk

Wisdom of the Bees, *Principles for Biodynamic Beekeeping* - by Erik Berrevoets

Honeybee Democracy - Thomas D. Seeley

WEBSITES

www.beeconscious.com - Website for Beeconscious, Ltd.

www.steinerbooks.org - Website for Anthroposophical media.

www.spikenardfarm.org - A bee sanctuary.

www.turtletreeseeds.com - A biodynamic seed initiative.

www.lilipoh.com - A lifestyle magazine for cultural creatives.

www.biodynamics.com - The biodynamic association website.

www.hawthornevalleyfarm.org - Educational center for biodynamic programs.

www.DrHauschka.com - A bee conscious skin care company.

www.themelissagarden.com - For a complete list of plants for honey bees.

www.truebotanica.com - Offers biodynamic supplements.

www.urielpharmacy.com - Online resource for remedies containing bee ingredients in homeopathic doses.

www.honeylocator.com - Find local slow honey. All honey is not the same!

www.3sistersinvest.com - Sustainable, socially responsible asset management.

www.svn.org - Transforming the way the world does business.

www.bioneers.org - Revolution from the heart of nature.

www.sweetbeginningsllc.com - Project facilitating rehabilitation of former prisoners through beekeeping.

www.longislandnn.org - A successful organic golf course.

www.growingsolutions.com - Information on organic golf courses.

www.spiritualschool.org - For those wishing to develop their connection to the Earth and learn the virtues and practicality of an interior, symbolic life.

www.changemyworldnow.com - An organization where teens discover how they can change the world *now.*

Every so often, a children's story comes along that is much, much more...

It is a message that touches the reality of a child's worldview. *Cassandra's Angel* has the power to be a lasting companion and give children and adults the confidence to become the people that they were meant to be.

www.CassandrasAngel.com